Fun with
AESOP

Volume I

Retold by Paul Tell   *Illustrated by* Connie Ross

Contents

For Alexander, my first grandson

Many thanks to those who helped bring this new approach
to Aesop's wisdom into being, especially for Dianna Williams'
editorial direction, Connie Ross's superb illustrations, and to
Denny & Pam Adams, Bob & Suanne Crowley, Marti Geise
and Becky Snyder for their skillful manuscript readings and
suggestions, and special thanks to the children ages four
through ten who responded as wide-eyed listeners to these
stories before the pictures were ever created!

TELCRAFT ®
A division of Tell Publications
Mogadore, Ohio 44260-0053

The Bundle of Sticks

One day a father lay sick in bed. He thought about the things he wanted his children to know.

There was one important lesson he wanted them to learn. So he called them to his bedside.

He asked the oldest to go and bring back some sticks and a string.

The children waited until the oldest returned. Their father then asked each to take a stick, put them together and tie them into a bundle. They wondered what their father would show them.

He started with the youngest. He told her to take the bundle of sticks in her hands and see if she could break them. She tried with all her might but couldn't break them.

The father asked the others to take a turn to see who might break the bundle. But none of them could break it, not even the oldest.

The father then told the oldest to untie the sticks, give one back to each of his brothers and sisters, and keep the last stick for himself.

"Now," said their father, "try to break them!"

Suddenly, the air filled with a crackling sound as all the sticks broke. Even the youngest was able to break her stick.

"Do you know the lesson this teaches?" asked their father.

What do you think their father was trying to teach them?

Together you are strong;
Separated you are weak.

Their father wanted them to
understand the importance of
staying together.

There's an old saying you might
try to remember:

United we stand,
divided we fall.

United means "together."
Divided means "separated."

Stay together, help each other,
and you'll be your strongest.

The Bundle of Sticks

Sticks,
 just sticks.
One by one
 you can break them.

Together?
 No. They won't break
When they're
 together!

But just separate them
 and see
How easily
 they will break!

So if you want to
 keep them strong,
Just put them all together;
Then whatever happens,
 they won't break.

If you care about and help each other,
then no problem will be too big.

DECLARATION

We, the undersigned, hereby agree to care about and help each other:

_____

_____

_____

_____

_____

_____

Seal

_____
Date

You will need: two sticks for each person in your group, a piece of string, a paper bag, a pencil, ruler and scissors.

Give two sticks to each person. Ask each of them to break one stick. Collect the remaining whole sticks and tie them into a bundle. Pass the bundle around and see if anyone can break it.

Ask everyone to repeat what the lesson teaches: "Together we are strong; separated we are weak."

A Declaration scroll may be cut from a paper bag. Write the words on the bag and use a ruler to draw the lines. Curl the ends around a pencil.

Have each person sign the scroll, then date it.

Tie the scroll to the bundle of sticks.

Using this same idea, a special gift could be made by using parchment paper for the scroll—and with a ribbon, tie the scroll to a bundle of cinnamon sticks.

The Crow and the Pitcher

What a hot, dry day, thought Johnny Crow. I think I'll die if I don't get something to drink!

Then Johnny saw a pitcher. It was standing near a well. He jumped up hopefully and stood on its brim. Looking down into it, he saw some water at the bottom.

You could almost hear him thinking: How wonderful that water looks. I must have some. I really must!

But try as he might, Johnny couldn't lean in far enough to reach the water. And all the while he was getting more and more thirsty!

He wasn't strong enough to tip the pitcher, and if he jumped inside he might not be able to fly back out. He thought and thought until he had a plan.

Then he jumped to the ground and picked up a pebble in his beak. He hopped back up and dropped it into the pitcher. He did this again and again, keeping his eye on the water.

He saw the water coming up little by little with every pebble he dropped. Good, he thought, but it's still too far down in the pitcher.

I know what I'll do. I'll keep on dropping in pebbles, more and more of them.

At last, after Johnny had dropped in many pebbles, the water came up high enough to reach.

Happily he drank until he was full!

How did Johnny get what he needed?

Johnny thought of a good idea, then,

Little by little,
without stopping,
he reached his goal.

Was Johnny's good idea, by itself,
enough to get the water he needed?

Think about it:
First,
Johnny *thought of* a good idea.
Then,
he *started doing it.*
And,
kept on doing it until finally he
could reach the water.

It is as simple as that.
Think of an idea.
Start doing it,
And keep on doing it
until it's done.

The Crow and the Pitcher

Mr. Crow,
   you cock your head
     and look.

What are you thinking?
   What do you want?
     I'd really like to know.

Water,
   just the thought of it
     makes me thirsty.

My mouth is so dry;
   my tongue feels
     like stone.

The sun is hot today
   and the road very dusty.
The trees are fortunate;
   they drink from far below.

Water, water,
   I must have some—
     I'm so thirsty!

There's a well, and a pitcher:
   an old glass pitcher
On the stones by the side
   of the well.

I'll take a look.
   Maybe someone left
     a little to drink.

Ooooh—I see some water,
   but I can't lean down
     far enough to reach it.

I know what I'll do.
   I'll drop in some pebbles—
Carry them in my beak,
   one at a time.

I see the water rising,
   very slowly;
With each pebble I drop,
   it gets a little higher!

Now I can reach it!
   What cool, clear water.
I'll throw my head back,
   let it trickle right down!

Name _____

Goal _____

Begin _____

Finish _____

You will need: a pencil and an idea or goal. Some ideas are: for five days do one helpful thing for someone else each day, learn a multiplication table, or something you can learn to do in about a week.

At the top fill in your name, your idea or goal, and the day you begin.

Draw a pebble in the mouth of the crow. Pretend that this will be the first of many pebbles he will drop into the pitcher. Draw a wavy line of water at the bottom of the pitcher. Above the water line draw a straight line and number it, "1."

On this line write notes about what you did today to help you toward reaching your goal. Draw a row of pebbles and a water line above your notes on line number "1."

Tomorrow draw another line above the water line, write number "2" on it and what you do that day. Then draw a row of pebbles and a water line above these notes.

Each day as you work toward your goal, continue to write notes and draw until your water reaches the top of the pitcher and you have finished what you wanted to do.

Write in the date you finish.

A Bell For The Cat

A family of mice lived in a big house with a very sly cat.

One day the mice held a meeting. "What can we do to protect ourselves from the cat?" they asked.

They talked, and after a while agreed that their biggest problem was the way the cat would quietly sneak up on them.

They decided they needed to know when the cat was coming. But HOW could they be warned?

It was quiet for a while as they tried to think of an idea.

"I've got it!" young Jeremy Mouse cried out. "I know what will warn us whenever the cat is coming!"

Jeremy had everyone's attention. Then lowering his voice, he told them his idea, as if he were letting them in on a secret. "Our warning," he said, "will be the sound of a bell!"

"A bell?" questioned the others.

"Yes, a BELL. I propose we tie a bell on a ribbon around the cat's neck. Whenever we hear the bell, we can run and hide until he has gone!"

"Hooray!" The mice cheered and clapped loudly. They thought this was a great idea, until . . .

Mr. Bishop, a very old mouse, stood up and raised his hand. Everyone became very quiet, more quiet than when young Jeremy was telling his idea.

Mr. Bishop had seen and thought about many things. In a voice just above a whisper, he spoke. "This all sounds very interesting, but WHO will tie the bell around the cat's neck?"

What can you learn from Jeremy and Mr. Bishop?

It's easy to think of ideas
you cannot do.

But once you learn *this* lesson,
quickly learn another:

Try to be wise like Mr. Bishop,
but also keep thinking
of new ideas like Jeremy!

It's true that not every idea will
work. But don't stop thinking of
new ideas.

Don't worry about suggesting an
idea that won't work. Some of the
best plans start with an impossible
idea, that is changed a little, into a
plan that will work.

One idea starts another idea.
So keep looking for ideas until you
find one you can use.

A Bell for the Cat

Now WHAT do you think
   of that?
Bells for kitties.
   It's a great idea.
Every cat
   should have one.
A bell for babies
   and their mamas
And their
   daddies too.
Yes, A BELL
   FOR ALL CATS,
The greatest idea
   yet.
Hooray for the
   well-being
Of all
   concerned mice.

Now at our house,
   we'll just take
A ribbon and a bell
   and tie it around the neck
      of that very sly cat!

Then we'll hear him coming
   every time.
We'll hear him coming
   and we'll run and hide
      until he has gone.

Yes, a great idea,
   a great idea.
But WHO, please tell me
   WHO will tie the bell
      to this cat?

You will need: a pencil, a piece of blank paper, scissors and a blindfold. This is played like "Pin the Tail on the Donkey."

Trace the bow in the picture on the piece of paper and cut it out. Lay your book flat on the table and put on the blindfold. Try to put the bow on the cat's neck. Take off the blindfold. How close did you come? Why did you have trouble? Should you keep trying or give up?

Is this an impossible situation or can you think of an idea that will work?

Try putting the bow on with the blindfold off. How close do you come this time? Why is this so? You might answer: First I could not see. And when I could, I solved my problem.

One problem the mice have is that the cat is too big. They might solve their problem by finding help from someone who is bigger than the cat.

Who will bell this cat?

You just did, without the blindfold!

Thank you, from Jeremy and all his friends.

The Rabbit and the Turtle

Sammy Rabbit was a runner. Lickety-split he'd dash from place to place.

"Sometimes I see a streak of gray and white from the corner of my eye," said Mr. Beaver to his wife.

"It's Sam Rabbit, I know!" said Mrs. Beaver. "I have seen it too, and when I look up he's already gone."

Sammy smiled when he heard them talk like this.

One day when the animals were gathered together, Sammy said to them, "I challenge anyone here to race with me."

Everyone grew quiet.

Then from way in the back a voice broke the silence:

"I accept your challenge."

The animals quickly turned to look. Much to their surprise they saw it was Jimmy Turtle speaking!

Now Sammy thought this was silly and laughed until he rolled on the ground. "What an easy race to win," he snickered.

Then getting up on one elbow, Sammy said, "I can't believe YOU would want to race. Why, I could run circles around you all the way, and still win!"

Now Jimmy was serious about racing. Looking Sammy right in the eye he said, "Wait 'til you've won before you say any more."

The other animals soon set up a running path.

At the starting line, Sammy wore a great big smile as he looked all around. But Jimmy kept looking straight ahead.

As Mr. Otter began the starting call, Sammy leaned back on his feet, ready to spring forward. Jimmy was quite different, standing low to the ground on all four feet. He didn't look much higher (or faster) than a rock with a flat bottom.

"Ready, set . . . GO!"
And the race began.

At the sound of "GO," dust flew everywhere as Sammy darted out ahead. Soon he was out of sight. The cloud began to settle and there walked Jimmy. It looked as though he'd hardly started!

After a while Sammy stopped. He felt good as he looked ahead and could see where the race would end.

Thinking he had plenty of time, Sammy decided to lie down for a nap on the soft, cool grass under a tree.

Jimmy never stopped. He just kept walking on his short, flat feet with a thump . . . thump . . . thump.

The bottom of his shell would sometimes bump the ground as he stepped into a hole or crawled over the root of a tree. But with his neck stretched out, he just kept walking, going on, and on, and on.

Later, Sammy woke up, rubbed his eyes and blinked a few times, not knowing how long he'd been asleep.

Suddenly, his eyes opened wide. No! There was Jimmy, about to cross the finish line!

Every muscle in Sammy wanted to jump up and run. But it was too late. Sammy was too far behind to catch up and win.

He stood frozen as he watched Jimmy finish with a thump . . . thump . . . thump.

Someone said they heard Jimmy say something as he crossed the line.

What do you think he said?

Slow and steady
wins the race.

The important thing
 is not
How *fast* you run.
 It's *not stopping*
 until you *finish*.

To finish a job,
 just get started
And keep going,
 and soon you
 will be done.

You pick up your room,
 one thing at a time,
Just as you walk
 to a friend's house,
 one step at a time.

18

The Rabbit and the Turtle

Rabbits like to run
   and play. Their feet
Are fast and fur is soft;
   what fun to
     see them run.

Turtles are nice
   in a different way.
Determined—they
   walk with stiffened steps
     and sway from side to side.

Rabbits dart
   when danger comes,
But a turtle tucks
   inside his shell and waits
     'til danger's passed.

Rabbits are fun
   to touch if you can;
While turtles are simply there,
   looking good at rest
     by a quiet pond.

You may be quick like a rabbit
   and maybe a little cute;
But don't forget, there are
   times to be like a turtle.
     Listen, it's true:

Steady walking
   beats running
And stopping—
   running
     and stopping.

You will need: a blank piece of paper, crayons, scissors, yarn or string, five comic strips from a newspaper and at least three people. A group can watch.

Trace the rabbit and turtle on to the paper. Color and cut them out. Give the rabbit to one person and the turtle to another. The person without a figure will be the otter who will start the race.

Set up a running path by stretching about two feet of string across a bulletin board or tie it between two chairs. The rabbit and the turtle persons can sit on the chairs. Mark string where the race will start and finish, and two "check points" in between. The rabbit and turtle will hang their figures on the string at the starting point with tape or paper clips.

The otter will cover up the words on one of the comic strips and explain the rules: The rabbit is to look at the pictures only and is not allowed to read the words. This person will go fast. The turtle is allowed to go slowly, to uncover and read all the words, quietly to himself. The otter will also read the strip silently (if you have a group let everyone read the comic). The otter will then ask the rabbit to tell the story. Everyone listening has to be quiet.

Don't give the rabbit clues by laughing!

When the rabbit is finished then the turtle will tell the story.

The otter will decide which story is closer to the story in the comic—if using a group, let them vote. The winner will move ahead to the first check point. Repeat with the next comic strip. The winner of each storytelling moves to the next check point along the way. Continue reading the comic strips and telling the stories until the rabbit or the turtle reaches the "finish line" and wins.

Who won your race? Who do you think will normally win this kind of contest, the rabbit—who goes fast and only looks at the pictures and guesses what the story is about—or, the turtle who goes slowly, who both reads the story and looks at the pictures?

Does someone in a hurry usually win, trying to go too fast?

Some good advice would be: Don't decide you cannot do something because you think you are not quick or smart enough. If you think you can't win, you won't. Also try not to be conceited about how fast or smart you are. You might think you will easily win and not pay enough attention, and then lose to someone who quietly keeps going. You might not even finish what you started to do.

The Donkey and the Lion's Skin

Once upon a time a donkey found a lion's skin which hunters had hung to dry in the sun.

"How exciting it would be to dress up and look like a lion!" said the donkey. Soon he was under the lion's skin and pulled it down over him.

As he walked toward the village everyone was afraid and started to run.

"What fun!" cried the donkey.

Feeling very pleased and proud of himself, the donkey lifted his head and let out a loud bra-a-a-ay.

Now this is not the sound that lions make, only donkeys!

A fox quickly turned back toward the donkey and said, "I know you by your voice."

What does this story tell us about trying to fool someone?

*Clothes may disguise us,
but when we talk,
Others will know who we
really are.*

A person who dresses up
to act like he is someone else
will soon be discovered for who
he really is when he begins
to talk!

The Donkey and the Lion's Skin

Donkeys see
  and donkeys do;
Yes, donkeys act
  as donkeys will.

Tell me to walk
  and I'll stand still;
Tell me to stand
  and off I'll go.

A lion's skin—
  how perfect
To make me into
  a kingly beast.

There, I've got it on!
  How great it feels,
And look how the
  others run!

I'm very important,
  strong and brave—
I'll raise my voice,
  make the others shake.

Bra-a-a-ay!
  Bra-a-a-a-a-ay!
Oops!   Now
  what have I done?

Oh, oh, my secret's out—
  first the fox,
Now all the others know
  I'm really a donkey!

You will need: a blank piece of paper, crayons, scissors, a paper plate, paste and string.

Trace the mask on the paper and cut it out. Paste it to a paper plate. Color the face brown or orange. Color in fur on the face. Color the paper plate yellow and snip it like fur. Cut out the eyes, and punch a hole in each side of face for string.

Cut and tie a string at each side.

Put the mask on and tie the strings at the back.

How do you feel? When you growl, do you see if others will run?

If you begin to talk, everyone will know you are not a lion—just as the fox knew the donkey was not a lion when he began to talk!

The Fox and the Grapes

One day a fox was walking through the woods. He saw some grapes hanging over a tree limb and his mouth began to water.

The grapes looked so good that he decided he must have some.

He jumped and jumped, springing up as high as he could. But try as he might, he couldn't jump high enough to reach them.

He quickly looked around to make sure that no one was watching. No clever fox will admit that he cannot do something.

Then in a desperate attempt, the fox started from way back and ran full speed to a new jumping spot. As he reached it he leaped into the air with all his might.

This time he came closer to the grapes, but still not close enough to snatch even one!

Very disappointed, he looked around once more just to be sure no one had seen him trying to reach the grapes. Then he walked away saying something to himself.

What do you think he said?

*I really didn't want
those grapes.
They must be very sour!*

Question:
   Do you think
      the grapes were sour?

The fox acted like people sometimes act:

   If a person can't have something
he wants, he may SAY he really
doesn't want it—he may even say
something is WRONG with it,
as if he would not want it at all.

26

The Fox and the Grapes

Grapes
   so purple,
Juicy,
   good.

They look so round and plump,
   ready to fall
And burst
   on the ground below.

My tongue is dripping
   and I must taste them
Before another moment
   passes.

Jump,
   jump!
Jump!
   Higher, higher!

I'll run and jump,
   with all my might,
To get those grapes
   so high.

Those grapes are
   really up there,
Far beyond
   my reach.

Well, I'll not waste
   another thought on them.
They must be
   very sour!

You will need: a blank piece of paper, a paper plate, crayons, scissors, paste and a big ribbon or bow.

Trace the fox and grape leaves on the piece of paper. Write your name on the fox. Write on the leaves the names of things you want but do not have. Color and cut out fox and leaves. Cut the center circle out of the paper plate to make a wreath. Paste the fox at the bottom of the paper plate wreath. Paste the leaves at the top. Make sure the fox cannot reach them.

Look at the fox and then read what is on the grapes. How do you feel about the things you want and cannot have?

Do you feel like the fox in the story? Do you need everything you want?

Now, all around your wreath write the names of good things that you already have. The fox would have been better off spending his time looking for food he could reach. By looking at what he couldn't have, he became unhappy. Learn to be satisfied with what you have. Be thankful, not greedy!

As you look at your wreath, notice that the things you have form a circle. The circle may have a special meaning to you—like a special ring. Maybe you truly have all you need. Put a bow at the top for decoration. Hang the wreath in your room.

About Me

My name _____

Date _____ Age _____

Grade ____ Teacher's name _____

School _____

My favorite school subject _____

What I want to be when I'm older _____

Best friends _____

_____

Favorite food _____

Favorite color _____

Hobbies—Sports _____

_____

My favorite Aesop's Fable _____

Why I like it best _____

Land of Aesop – I

Color Design by: _____

Age: _____